CW01426130

THE RHYMOLOGY ANTHOLOGY

THE RHYMOLOGY ANTHOLOGY

GLEN BRADY-POWER

THE PAPER HOUSE
PUBLISHING

Copyright © 2024 by Glen Brady-Power

All rights reserved.

No part of this book may be reproduced in any form or by any electronic or mechanical means, including information storage and retrieval systems, without written permission from the author, except for the use of brief quotations in a book review.

To all my loved ones

CONTENTS

ONE
THE RAVEYARD

It was a cold and depressing full-moon night

The giant glowing moon kept the whole town bright,

My wife had recently just died,

And for the last few weeks I cried and I cried.

I drank so much liquor to ease the pain,

And I began my walk to the graveyard in the pouring rain.

Soon after the rain started, arrived the thunder and lightning,

But I was too depressed and too drunk to consider it frightening.

My wife's death had brought me so much grief,

That to even sit by her grave brought me some form of relief,

1

Just being near her helped ease my sorrow,

However, a life without her gave no hope for tomorrow.

I reached her grave and put some fresh flowers by her headstone,

I told her that I would never move on and that I'd spend the rest of my life alone.

Then I heard a sound that sounded like a record play,

Then I heard it being scratched in a particular way,

It sounded like it was being scratched by a professional DJ.

I turned around to see who else was there as I had thought I was alone,

And there stood a dapper skeleton with his mixing board. "Hello, my name is DJ Groovy Bones!

I'm the DJ of the dead,

Instead of lying in your coffins all night, get up and dance instead,

All you dead folk, get up and groove; this ain't no graveyard,

Cos anytime DJ Groovy Bones arrives, this place becomes the Raveyard!"

And suddenly, the ground began to shake,

I thought it was some kind of earthquake,

And then it cracked and began to break,

The once-sleeping corpses were now awake.

These zombies crawled out from the ground,

And began raving to the sound,

My wife was there,

With her long brown hair,

But she was missing her skin and missing her nose,

And only tatters remained of her clothes,

I gave her a hug and I gave her a kiss,

She said, "The Raveyard is an occasion you just can't miss."

So we raved in the graveyard,

Around all the graves in the Raveyard,

And my God, we raved hard.

DJ Groovy Bones kept on DJing,

We loved all the tunes that he was playing,

The zombies were all bopping while decaying,

When he threw on each song, we were all hurraying,

The songs were so loud I couldn't hear what my wife was saying,

But to each song we kept on singing,

The hype was surreal and my ears were ringing.

DJ Groovy Bones then said, "I only perform for the dead,

I know you think you're alive instead,

But the matter of fact is you bit the led,

A life without your wife had too much dread,

So you put a bullet through your head,

If you were alive, you couldn't see this,

It's far too strange for mortal eyes to witness."

Then it all flashed before my eyes,

Through the depression and the cries,

That I had caused my own demise.

I remembered putting the gun up to my mouth,

Then I noticed a hole in the back of my head with blood pouring out.

Now I'm reunited with my wife,

I much prefer the afterlife,

I might be dead, but I'm still alive,

Just not to those with mortal eyes,

And though I do sleep most of the year,

I come alive each time I hear,

That beautiful ringing in my ear,

The sound that makes all of us zombies cheer,

When the music lets you know DJ Groovy Bones is near.

TWO
CONNY 2-HANDS

Conny 2-Hands is the man with the plan.

He's willing to fight any woman or man,

"Step right up," Conny shouts aloud,

"I'm willing to scrap anyone," he then says to the crowd,

"If you can last a minute, I will pay you a grand,

But I'll knock anyone out when I start throwin' these hands."

People formed a line as they all wanted the money,

But when Conny started throwing hands, the results were not funny.

He kept knocking everyone out after one second, two seconds, three seconds, four;

There was one body, two bodies, three bodies, more.

The truth of the matter is if he catches you with a left or a right,

You will either be dead or unconscious for the rest of the night.

Conny stood there proud in the middle of Dublin Square,

He said, "Anyone else wanna scrap? Challenge me if you dare!"

A giant man stepped up, he was 7ft 3,

Conny knocked him out cold with a left, right, and then a knee.

Conny then said, "I'll fight anything, anytime, anywhere,

There was then a huge beam of light, and Conny flew through the air.

He did not know what was happening;

why the hell was he flying?

He believed he was going to heaven;

he genuinely thought he was dying.

But the beam of light then brought him back to the ground,

But wherever he landed was like no normal town.

There were pyramids and slaves that were all getting whipped,

Conny then realized he was in ancient Egypt,

The people all bowed as they were in the presence of Tutankhamun,

But Conny stayed standing and said, "I ain't bowing for you!"

They all gasped in shock, Tutankhamun said in Egyptian, "What did you say?!"

Conny somehow understood him and said, "If you think you'll make me bow, man, I'll knock your ass out right away!"

Tutankhamun's guards tried to attack Conny,

Conny hit them both with cheeky jabs to the body

A left uppercut to the left guard and a right uppercut to the right, It is needless to say they were out cold for the night.

He then beat anyone else that tried to oppose,

By hitting, and kicking, and throwing and elbowing them.

It was just Conny and Tutankhamun left, Tut said,

"Please don't hurt me!"

Conny then said, "Sorry man," and hit him a one, two, and a three.

Anubis then stepped out from the pyramid, the half jackal half man,

Conny then said, "Remember my name, boy, they call me Conny 2-Hands!"

Conny hit him with an overhand right and a left kick to the head.

He then looked around as everyone in Egypt was either unconscious or dead.

Conny was then sucked through a portal into a whole other place,

He was now on top of 'Mount Olympus', with the Greek Gods staring at his face.

There was Zeus, Poseidon, and Hades, they all said, "Who are you?"

He again said, "They call me Conny 2-Hands, and I'm about to whoop all of you too!"

'Zeus' the God of lightning and thunder,

When they started throwing down he realized he had made a blunder.

Conny 2-Hands knocked Zeus out cold,

Hades said, "If I whoop your ass, Conny, then I'm taking your soul!"

Conny said, "Fine, come at me, old man!"

Conny then broke Hades' neck with a suplex slam.

Poseidon said, "Those are my brothers, you fool, prepare to be beat!"

Conny then said, "One thing I'll never taste is the taste of defeat!"

Conny swiped his two legs and took him to the ground,

Got in a top mount position and gave him a ground and pound,

Conny then said, "I'm by far the toughest guy around!"

Conny then transported back to the age before time,

Back before anything, no laws, and no crime.

There stood the dinosaurs, and over stomped the mighty T-Rex,

Conny shouted, "Take one more step, pal, and I will break your neck!"

The T-Rex then began to run toward him,

Conny caught the T-Rex with a single-leg takedown and absolutely floored him.

Conny then got the T-Rex's short arm in an armbar,

You could hear the beast's roar, so wide and so far.

He broke the T-Rex's arm,

And then smashed out his teeth to do further harm.

He killed the T-Rex and then moved on to the others;

He killed all of T-Rex's sisters and brothers,

He killed all the Brontosaurus, Carnotaurus, and Spinosaurus,

To put a long story short, he killed off any type of aurus.

The dinosaurs were done with, and again, he was transported through time,

The year was 2800, and the aliens were in control of Earth, with their powers so divine.

The alien chief commanded, "Seize that human!"

Conny said, "I'm Conny 2-Hands, and I'll knock you out too, man!"

These aliens had powers and tried to use telekinesis,

But it did not work on Conny, as he smashed their jaws to pieces.

"Come over here, fella," Conny said to the alien chief,

"And trust me when I say this will only be brief."

The alien chief said, "Be prepared, Conny, you are about to die."

Conny caught him with a flying knee straight into the eye.

Out of nowhere, things began coming out from the ground,

There were robots, and gladiators and demon hellhounds,

And four men on horses that said, "We are the horsemen of the apocalypse,"

Conny said in return, "I'll batter you soft boys if you keep running your lips!"

"Come at me, boys!" Conny shouted, "I can do this all day!"

One after another, Conny put them away.

He caught one gladiator with an elbow and another in a triangle choke,

He took out a hellhound with a double eye poke.

He took out the four horsemen through the use of karate,

He shouted at the others, "You still want a piece of me?!"

A robot approached him; Conny said, "Wanna see a trick?"

Conny did a backflip and hit him with a Capoeira kick.

He took out another with an uppercut to the chin,

Conny laughed out, "Did you really think you'd win?"

He tossed down another with a special kind of throw,

One that he had learned through studying Aikido.

He had destroyed every challenge, everyone was defeated,

They were dead and unconscious, and all were depleted.

A voice rang out from the clouds in the sky,

God said, "Conny 2-Hands, you're the number 1 guy."

God reached his hand down and put a crown on Conny's head,

God shouted, "You're the king of the world, Conny, and by you the world shall be led."

A throne then appeared right before Conny's eyes,

And as he sat down on his throne, he did not look one bit surprised.

The world all chanted, you could hear the voices sing,

They sang out, "All hail Conny 2-Hands, for he is our king."

THREE

THE TALE OF MAGGIE CREEK

Did you ever hear the tale of Maggie Creek?

Well, Maggie had a humungous pimple on her cheek.

It was the size of a football, and as hard as led,

And she struggled to sleep with it, when she lay in her bed.

She went to the doctor, and he gave her ointment,

But it didn't get rid of it, to her disappointment.

She would pull it, and pinch it, and squeeze it each day,

But it simply made no difference; it just would not go away.

She tried steaming her face to open her pours,

And would spend hours each day researching cures.

She tried jumping face-first into a wall,

But it didn't make a difference to her giant pimple at all.

She asked her friend to stamp on it to see what that would do,

But it didn't make a difference, and day by day, it grew.

It became absolutely ginormous, and circular and plump,

In fact, it was far too big to be a pimple or lump.

So she finally went to the hospital and was put into A and E,

She cried, "Please remove this feckin' thing, even if I need surgery!"

The surgeon used his stethoscope, and he could not believe what he had found.

He screamed, "This is absolutely crazy, but her face needs an ultrasound!"

The surgeon literally passed out,

Maggie freaked out and cried.

As the scan that they did on her face found a baby inside.

Her cheek then began to leak, her water had just broke.

The midwife said, "You're going into labour!" Maggie thought this all must be a joke.

But this was no joking matter, and the midwife began to give Maggie's cheek a squeeze,

The pain of labour was surreal, Maggie fell to her knees.

The midwife then said, "You're gonna need a C section, but this time 'C' stands for 'Cheek,'

And might I just add, you're quite the freak, missus Creek!"

They then opened the giant pimple-like bump on her face

And out came the baby to her mother's embrace.

She named her daughter 'Tonya,' Little Tonya Creek,

Or, to most people, 'The child that came out of a cheek.'

FOUR
THE BOXER WITH NO ARMS

Sammy wanted to be a boxer,

He had the toughness and charms,

But he was different from all other boxers,

For he had no arms.

He joined the local boxing club,

No one gave him a chance,

All except for one,

A man named James Lance.

He said, "You wanna be a boxer kid?

Then here's what we'll do,

You'll meet me here at 6 am tomorrow,

And I'll give you the run-through."

And so the next morning arrived,

And Sammy was there right on time,

James said, "I don't think you'd show up, kid.

Now stand on that line."

He made Sammy do sprints, he could run all day,

James laughed aloud,

"You're like a young David Haye!"

"You'll be a great boxer son, I just have a hunch,

There are ways to win boxing matches,

Without throwing a punch."

James had an idea,

He had a few tricks up his sleeve,

He was going to teach Sammy

How to dodge, bob, and weave.

They trained each day,

His reflexes became insane,

Purely phenomenal defense,

Was instilled in his brain.

They upped his training regime,

Bit by bit each day,

James would even shoot at Sammy,

But he would just slip out of the way.

They had now trained for years,

Now Sammy sought competition,

To become the World Champion,

Was now his life's mission.

The boxing world champion,

Had accepted a fight,

And after a grueling training camp,

His opponent pulled out on the night.

The champion was eager to defend his title,

He said, "I will fight whoever is willing to step in!"

Sammy jumped out from the crowd and screamed,

"I'll fight you, and I bet I will win!"

The champion laughed, As did the crowd,

They all scoffed, and giggled,

And mocked Sammy aloud.

However, Sammy was not alone,

For he had coach James by his side;

James loved Sammy's bravery,

And he felt nothing but pride.

The champion found this hysterical, "A boxer with no arms?

But he can't throw a punch, Or do any harm?

A boxer without the ability to box, Is like a pair of feet,

Without the ability to wear socks,

But if you're willing to fight,

Then I'll just knock you out,

I doubt anyone else is willing to take this bout."

And so the fight began 'DING DING.'

Sammy was dancing and flowing around the ring,

The champion started to throw powerful shots at Sammy's head,

And if one had landed, Sammy would've been dead,

But the shots wouldn't land,

Sammy just kept on moving,

He was swaying, and bobbing, and dancing, and grooving,

The champ grew frustrated. He was crying while swinging,

Sammy began whistling, and humming, and singing,

Sammy laughed out, "I can do this all day!"

The champ threw an uppercut, but Sammy jumped out of the way,

Sammy was laughing, "Is that all you got?!

Keep throwing punches, I'll just dodge the lot!"

The champ kept throwing, he was panting, and tired,

Whereas Sammy was electric, like he had just been wired,

The champ mustered up all his energy, and he threw one more,

And the exhaustion set in, and he bundled to the floor,

He passed out right there, Sammy won the bout,

It went down as a technical knockout,

Sammy was now the boxing world champ,

And in the history books, you'll find his name stamped,

The once mocking crowd were now his fans,

"Sammy!" They chanted, "You're the man!"

Coach James cried out, "It's not your lack of arms that sets you and everyone else apart,

It's what you've got inside you, boy, you've got the most heart!"

FIVE
THE PAINTING

It was the opening night of the brand-new art gallery,

So much wonderful artwork in the town of Lochnee.

There were sculptures, and drawings, and paintings go leor,

And this ginormous art gallery had twenty-five floors.

Each floor filled with artwork, covering every inch of every wall,

Every doorway was covered with artwork, even every hall.

Everyone was dumbfounded by this wonderful display,

And most curious of all was a man named 'Todd Gray.'

He walked through every hallway and admired all the art,

And he eyeballed a sculpture of a giant marble love heart.

There was graffiti art covering one of the floors,

And hilarious comedic sketches covering some of the doors.

There were woodwork carvings, and metalworks, too,

And a technology room with some inventions that were new.

Todd observed every room, and every hallway, and door,

And then he finally arrived on the twenty-fifth floor.

This floor was quite strange, it was almost completely bare,

Just one painting on the wall, it was of a man in a chair.

Todd had a look, this painting was nothing unique,

Why was it here? It was just rather bleak.

A man then approached Todd, the only other man on that floor,

He said, "You can look at this painting for 5 minutes, but not for a split second more."

Todd asked the man, "What did you say?"

The man said, "Not a second more than 5 minutes, okay, Mr. Gray?"

"Mr. Gray?" Todd wondered, how did he know his name?

He had never met him before. Was this some kind of game?

Todd turned around to ask the man, then things got quite weird,

For somehow, the man had just disappeared.

Todd was now curious about what the man had said,

And he couldn't get it out of his head.

So he set a timer for five minutes and one second time,

And he planned to stare at the painting until he heard his phone chime.

So he stared at the painting of the man in the chair,

But nothing was happening, the painting still looked quite bare.

Then his alarm chimed, and over five minutes had gone by,

"Why did the man say all that?" Todd really couldn't understand why.

Then something strange happened, something he couldn't explain,

He began to panic. Was there something wrong with his brain?

Todd tried to scream, he tried to cry,

But his mouth wouldn't move; he couldn't understand why.

He tried to blink, but all he could do was stare,

Todd was inside the painting; he was now the man in the chair.

SIX

ALAN KOHOLICOVIC

Alan Koholicovic was born in 1953,

In a small little village, to a middle-class family.

Ever since he was born, ever since he could think,

He had always had an addiction to drink.

He came out of his mother holding a bottle of wine,

The doctors couldn't understand it but said the baby was fine.

His first word was "vodka," then he begged his parents to give him a shot,

His mother burst into tears and screamed, "I absolutely will not!"

They asked a psychologist, he said, "Try not to fear."

Until Alan screamed, "Where the hell do you keep your beer?!"

The psychologist tried to hypnotize Alan, to get drink out of his head,

But it didn't work on Alan, he just begged for a shot of tequila instead.

The hospital ran some tests on Alan's brain,

They couldn't find anything, then he cried out for champagne.

They then ran some more tests, and what they found was terribly strange,

It was downright crazy, it was completely deranged.

He had absolutely no blood, he had alcohol instead,

Alcohol running straight from his toes, right up to his head.

It made no sense to anyone, how was he not dead?

This baby needed a different kind of bottle to be fed.

So they fed him more alcohol to keep him hydrated,

But the amount of alcohol he needed was more than they anticipated.

He drank every bottle, and every crate, in every store,

But he cried, and he cried, and he just wanted more.

His small little village was going through an alcohol drought,

As it had all been consumed through Alan Koholicovic's mouth.

At this point, Alan was just two years old,

Continuously begging for a brew that was ice cold.

The pubs all closed, as every last drop had been taken from the tap,

Poor little Alan was such a thirsty young chap.

People were dying for a drink, but the stock wasn't due for two weeks,

And the hope for getting drunk had become very bleak.

However, one day, Alan sneezed, and out from his nose,

Spewed alcohol, like some kind of alcohol hose.

People gathered round and held out their hands,

As Alan shot out any drink they wanted on command.

A whiskey for one, and a tequila for another,

A cold beer for his father, and a wine for his mother,

A vodka for his neighbour, a cider for the teacher,

A little bit of brandy to the local preacher.

The doctor had a gin and tonic, the nurse had a cocktail,

Little Alan Koholicovic gave alcohol to every woman and male.

They all said cheers, you could hear their glasses clink,

And they all thanked Alan for all of the drink.

SEVEN
A FREAKS HALLOWEEN

Do you remember trick or treating as a child?

Do you remember the laughter and how much you smiled?

It was so fun to dress up as anything you wanted,

Like Spider-Man, or Superman, or anything that's haunted

Can you remember the thrill as your bag filled with treats?

And all that amazing sugar for you to eat.

Running wild through the neighborhood with all of your friends,

And always looking forward to next year as soon the night ends.

Well, unfortunately this wasn't the case for little Mikey Brown,

And Halloween was always a time that made him frown.

See, poor Mikey Brown wasn't your typical kid,

And he had no friends, but he always wished that he did.

His parents were always so mean to him too,

As were the kids at school, poor Mikey didn't know what to do.

He wasn't into the things that the others enjoyed,

And being different from the others, made the others annoyed.

His parents would also shout, "Why can't you just be like all the other kids?

We wish we never had you!" And poor Mikey wished they never did.

This story, however, is one that is true, but it's just so obscene,

That you wouldn't even think of it in your wildest of dreams.

Mikey: It all happened ten years ago on the night of Halloween,

And as per usual everyone was being mean.

My mother shouted at me, "Go out trick or treating, see what you can bring me back."

And my father shouted, "Yeah, hurry up, and by the way, we get all of your snacks!"

I know you might think they were just kidding, but they never did,

They were always horrible to me, their useless little kid.

So, I went upstairs and pulled out the drawer on the second shelf

And I put on the vampire costume, that I made all by myself.

Everyone else had costumes bought for them, by their caring mam and dad,

Unfortunately, that's something I longed for, but something I never had.

I wore a bin bag as a cloak, and wore jam as blood,

I used two white pencils as my fangs, and in the mirror, I stood.

I looked absolutely ridiculous, nothing at all like a vampire,

But hey, what could I do? At least God loves a trier.

I went downstairs and they laughed at me. "What kind of costume is that?

You look nothing like Count Dracula, you just look like a twat!"

I had gotten used to it, this was nothing new,

They just loved being mean to me, it was their favorite thing to do.

So, I walked outside and off I set, I went from door to door,

I could sense the people judging my costume, it hurt me to my core.

But anyway, I continued on my way,

It was sad walking on my own, as I could see all the other children play.

But I was nothing at all like them, and they were nothing like me,

That's just how my life was, no friends or loving family.

Maybe I was just a freak,

Too small, too flimsy, and too weak,

But that wasn't my fault, not my fault at all,

I couldn't make myself stronger,

I couldn't make myself tall,

I couldn't make myself enjoy what everyone else did,

Just because I didn't love sports, didn't make me less of a kid!

I kept on walking, trick or treating from door to door,

And then I realized I was in a place I had not seen before,

I was completely lost, all on my own,

And I couldn't contact anyone, I didn't have a phone,

But even if I did, who would I have called?

No one cared in the slightest about me at all.

So I knocked on the only door that I could see,

And a man opened the door, he was dressed just like me,

Well, sort of, his costume was a lot better than mine,

He had great fake fangs; they were as big as a lions.

I told him I was lost, and he said, "Come inside, you must be freezing."

I said that I was okay, and then I started sneezing.

He laughed. "Oh goodness, I think you might be getting a cold,

You poor little thing, blood bless your soul,

My name is Vinny, Vinny Vampire,

Let's get you warmed up by our blazing fire,

Come into the sitting room, meet my family."

And when I went in they all said "hi" to me.

They were all in great costumes, they all looked so legit,

If they'd entered a best costume competition, they would've won it.

So, they all introduced themselves one by one,

"Hello, my name's Pumpkin Head I'm Papa Vampire's son"

"Hi, I'm Jared, Jared the Scarecrow,

I'm Pumpkin Head's uncle and Vampires bro,

And this is my wife, Sydney, Sydney Shotgun,

But don't worry, she ain't angry, so she won't shoot anyone!"

"Not yet anyway" Sydney laughed,

"Sorry about my husband, the guy's pretty daft."

And then the Vampire man introduced his wife,

He said, "This is Valentina, Valentina the Knife,

The most amazing Knifewoman I've ever met in my life,

Or in my death for that matter!"

Valentina then said, "Sorry, after a few glasses of blood, he's as mad as a hatter!"

I then introduced myself and said, "Hi, I'm Mikey, Mikey Brown,

And your costumes are by far the coolest I've ever seen around."

They then paused for a moment and began laughing with glee,

And what happened next absolutely terrified me,

Vinny Vampire turned into a bat and began flying around the room,

I then realized these people were not wearing costumes,

They really were monsters, just like they said,

Then Pumpkin Head boy pulled off his head,

And Jared the scarecrow pulled out his insides,

I bolted towards the front door, but it was locked, so I ran upstairs to hide.

I ran into the first room, and hid under the bed,

And I cried as I feared that soon I'd be dead.

That was it, I was done for, my life had come to an end,

A fitting ending for someone with no loved ones or friends,

I was shaking with fear as I heard them walk up the stairs,

I was a helpless fly trapped in this evil family's lair.

I began crying as I was pulled out from under the bed,

And just when I thought I was about to be dead,

They all hugged me, and began stroking my head,

And Vinny Vampire looked at me and said,

"It's okay, Mikey, there's no need to fear,

It's no coincidence that you wound up here,

We know that in your life everyone is cruel,

You have horrible parents, and you're bullied at school,

We know everything, Mikey, that's why you are here,

We want to end your hardship, we want to bring you cheer,

I know they all say you're a freak, we know that you're an outcast,

But now that you're here, you can have a happy life at last,

Because we are all outcasts, we were treated like freaks too,

There's not much of a difference between us and you,

We're not bad people; we're just misunderstood,

But the way we've been treated is not very good.

So, this is why we live here, this is an outcast society,

And we want you to live here, we'll be your family.

We'll love you like real family should,

And I promise I'll never try to drink your blood!"

He began to laugh, as did I too,

And as I looked at them all, at that moment I knew,

That this was exactly where I was meant to be,

And I live there to this day, with my true family.

EIGHT
WINSTON BLARE'S BOOKSHELF

Pat was a cleaner, and he was starting his new job,

He was going to clean for Winston Blare, a multi-billionaire snob.

Winston gave Pat the run-through of all the things that needed to be done,

Before he returned from his meeting, he'd be back at ten to one.

He said:

You must clean all the windows,

You must clean all the walls,

You must dust all the doorways,

You must scrub all the halls,

You must polish my ornaments,

You must hoover the stairs,

You must assort all my socks,

Into their matching pairs,

But there's one thing that you must never touch,

There's one thing that I clean myself,

You better not dare to touch it,

Stay away from my wonderful bookshelf.

The bookshelf was Winston's pride and joy,

He had been collecting rare books ever since he was a boy.

He had many first editions, many of which were signed,

Some were the most expensive books you could find.

He purchased one at an auction for one million pounds,

It was the only copy of the book that was still around.

Winston then gave Pat a glare,

And he pierced his soul with an ice-cold stare.

He then said in a deep, and unnerving tone

"You will regret it if you don't leave my bookshelf alone!"

He then slammed the door, and left Pat by himself,

And his curiosity was growing about Winston's bookshelf.

Pat then cleaned all the windows,

He cleaned all the walls,

He dusted the doorways,

And scrubbed all the halls.

He polished the ornaments,

He hoovered the stairs,

And he assorted all the socks,

Into their matching pairs.

He wrote a line through everything that Winston had asked,

He had nothing else to complete, no more tasks.

But there was one thing in his head that would not go away,

The thoughts of that bookshelf were leading his mind astray.

He began to sweat heavily, as he grew in frustration,

He tried to resist the bookshelf's temptation.

He fought as hard as he could, but the temptations grew stronger and stronger,

Until he eventually stopped resisting, he couldn't fight the temptation any longer.

He shuffled his way over to the sacred bookshelf,

And he looked around to ensure that he was all by himself.

The books looked phenomenal, they were so beautiful and old,

And the bookshelf was made of pure solid gold.

He reached out and grabbed a book, like you'd do in a bookstore,

And he dropped down 20 feet through a trap door in the floor.

He couldn't believe it, he screamed, and he cried,

As he noticed five other dead cleaners inside.

As they say, curiosity killed the cat,

The same rule applied to the other cleaners and Pat.

NINE
THE COW-BOY

Ever since he was a young child, Larry had a dream,

He wanted to be the animal known for its cheese, milk, and cream.

He wanted to be a cow and live out in the field,

He wanted to have grass each day as his meal.

He would run around his house screaming, "Moo moo moo."

His father would ask, "Larry, what's wrong with you?"

Larry would say, "When I grow up, I'm going to be a cow."

His mother would respond, "Larry, don't be stupid, snap out of it now!"

But he didn't snap out of it no matter how hard everyone pleaded,

He simply believed that being a cow was something that he needed.

He would paint his face with patches of black and white,

And while asleep, he would dream of cows all through the night.

His teacher asked him, "When you grow up, what is it you will do?"

Larry then said, "I shall stand still in a field, and occasionally,

I'll MOOO!"

His parents decided to bring little Larry to see a doctor,

His obsession with being a cow was strange to her and shocked her.

But she told the parents that "it's just a phase, he'll grow out of it."

But if we look back on it now, she was not right one bit.

He decided that when he got older, he would change his name to 'Daisy,'

And that he simply could not wait to be a big cow and be lazy.

He could not wait until the day he could be in a field all day long,

And when his parents would give out about it, he'd say, "I'm doing nothing wrong."

When Larry reached 18, he changed his name by Deed Poll to 'Daisy.'

His parents went ballistic: "Larry, what the hell?! Are you crazy?!"

He said, "I'm not crazy I'm just determined to be a cow,

And now's the time, I've had enough, I'm going to do it now!"

He went upstairs and gathered sheets, wood, and fur to create his costume,

And then he put it all together right there in his room,

And then he colored it in black and white using lots of paint,

And when he walked downstairs in his costume it made his mother faint.

His dad shouted, "Larry, that's it, I've had enough of you!"

And in return, Larry stared at him and let out one big "MOOOOO."

He then ran out of his house excited,

It was finally time to be a cow and he was delighted.

He ran and ran until he came across a huge field of cows with tonnes of hay,

His legs were now so weary as he had been running all day,

So now it was time to rest and in the field is where he lay.

In the morning, the farmer came and threw them all some grain,

Larry thought, *Wow, this is so delicious, it's insane!*

Then the farmer let them into another field, and they began to run around,

Larry began to eat some grass straight up from the ground.

He then began to play and roll around in the mud,

Being a cow felt even better than he thought it would,

He played and ate so much grass, grain, and hay,

He did this so so often, in fact, he did it every day.

He had gotten so fat that his belly touched the floor,

But he just ate more and more and a little bit more.

Then the farmer came out to the field, and he lined up all the cows,

He picked out the biggest ones, including Larry and said, "Okay, come along now."

He gathered the bunch into the wagon and off they set,

Larry thought they were going someplace fun, but this was a journey he would regret,

They then reached the slaughterhouse and Larry realised that this place meant death.

He tried to scream, and he tried to shout,

He tried to tell the farmer this was a mistake. "Please, sir, let me out!"

Then the farmer walked up to him and said, "Quit your cryin'!

Why did you want to be a cow if you're afraid of dyin'?

Ya see, Larry, your parents rang a few months back to see if you dropped by,

I knew it was you all along, but I thought it would be funnier if I lied,

So, I told them no, I hadn't seen you, but I'd ring them if I did,

I thought I'd have fun with the cow wannabe, you're quite the idiot kid."

Larry said, "Wait, you mean you know I'm not a cow?!

Then why the hell did you bring me here?! Let me out now!"

The farmer said, "But Larry, being a cow was your choice to make,

What made you think it wouldn't result in you being a sirloin steak?

Anyway, I informed the abattoir that you'd be slaughtered here today,

He just laughed and said, 'Hahaha, what a great idea,' and had nothing more to say,

So come on, kid, you wanted to live as a cow, now are you prepared to go out that way?"

Larry thought for a moment, then said, "I'm ready to die, I'll give you my reason if you'd like to know why?"

You see, my whole life, being a cow was my dream,

Now it's fulfilled, so slaughter me if you wish, and I will not even scream."

The farmer said, "I like your bravery kid, is there any last thing you'd like me to do?"

Larry simply stared and smiled and let out one last "MOOOOOOOOOOOO."

The farmer smiled back at him, in fact, he shed a tear,

And he looked into Larry's eyes and saw he had no fear.

Larry was then slaughtered, but it all felt okay,

He chose to live life as a cow and to also go out that way.

TEN
THE BOSS

Do you ever find yourself frustrated when you get home from work?

Do you ever find yourself questioning, "Why is my boss such a jerk?"

Well, did you ever wonder if your boss's boss treats him poorly too?

And maybe that's why your boss is taking all his frustrations out on you?

Well, what about your boss's boss's boss? Maybe he's the same,

Maybe he's just really mean and drives your boss's boss insane.

But what makes him so horrible? Maybe his boss makes him cry,

Maybe he won't leave him alone, and he doesn't know why.

Well, what about your boss's boss's boss's boss's boss?

The man where it all stems from, the man named Mr. Joss.

He was the boss of everybody, every single one,

He bossed everyone around, didn't his job sound rather fun?

He had no-one to answer to, because he had no boss,

He told people what to do, and he didn't give a toss.

He had a finger in every pie,

And made all your boss's boss's boss's boss cry,

He would spend all day screaming down the phone,

And wouldn't leave your boss's boss boss alone,

All his anger really messed with people's brains,

And it drove your boss's boss's boss boss insane.

And the list goes on and on and on,

Every Paddy and every John,

Anyone that cried because of their boss,

It all linked back to Mr. Joss.

Until one day, Mr. Joss, spotted the most beautiful woman he ever did see,

And he mustered up the courage and asked, "Will you go on a date with me?"

The woman agreed, and they went on a date,

To a fancy restaurant, and ate finished all on their plates,

They dated many times, she was his angel from above,

And it was a thing of true beauty, as they fell madly in love.

Soon after that, he made her his wife,

And then everything began to change in his life.

If he'd stay out too late, without calling home,

She'd blow a fuse and root through his phone,

If he didn't clean up, or do what she said,

You would literally see steam shooting out of her head.

She would kick her feet up while he did the chores,

And she'd go bananas if he left open any doors,

His whole life was controlled now, he felt so run down,

Life was so draining being bossed around.

He was no longer the boss of everyone,

And he now understood being bossed around isn't fun.

So, if you are ever being screamed at while at work,

And if you can't understand why your boss is a jerk,

And you wanted to know, who it is that you should blame,

At least you know the answer, and Mrs. Joss is her name.

ELEVEN

BILLY BOB'S BIG BANG BEARD

Did you ever hear the tale of Billy Bob's Big Bang Beard?

Well, let me just warn you: this story is very weird.

It's a true story, or so I have heard,

Although maybe not, it seems too absurd.

There was a man called Billy Bob, he was nice and shy,

And pretty much, an all-round normal kind of guy.

Except for one thing, he had a big white beard,

But that's not the part that makes this tale weird.

You see, the beard kept on growing, it grew down past his feet,

And it covered his mouth, the poor man couldn't eat.

He was severely dehydrated, as he could no longer drink,

He became quite delusional, until he could no longer think.

Why didn't he cut his beard? You might ask,

Well, cutting this beard was an impossible task.

His beard was like titanium, you couldn't cut through it,

He was losing the will to live, and the rest of the town knew it.

They fed him on a drip, as his beard kept growing.

And it made the whole town look like it had been snowing.

It grew and it grew at a terrifying rate,

And the town tried to stop it before it was too late.

But there wasn't a single thing that the townsfolk could do,

The beard simply grew, and it grew, and it grew.

His beard smothered the whole town, and they all disappeared,

I did warn you at the start that this story was weird.

But it didn't stop there, It didn't stop anywhere,

It ran through his country, it smothered everyone,

The beard was a narcissist; it was having so much fun.

It moved onto other countries, eating everyone up,

But its hunger kept growing, it could not get enough.

It covered the world, and the universe too,

Swallowing everything whole, never needing to chew.

It got so ginormous that the beard then imploded,

Causing a massive big bang when it exploded.

That massive big bang started a new universe,

That was run by dinosaurs and other things first.

As time went by, things started to change,

And the food chain began to rearrange.

And finally, we wound up in the world of today,

I bet you didn't think the Big Bang happened that way.

TWELVE
POKER AT MIDNIGHT MANSION

When the clock strikes twelve in the Midnight Mansion,

There comes a drastic change and a huge expansion.

Up until midnight, it's a normal house,

But once it hits midnight you'll feel as small as a mouse.

Once the bells began ringing the monsters came to play,

They loved playing card games in their own special way.

They would play Go-Fish and Snap and games never heard of,

Like Swipzies and Trickziez and another called Zwirlov.

These games had no badness, no arguing, no fighting, not one!

No adult-rated madness, just pure childish fun.

They loved one another, they were all best of friends,

The kind of friendships you'd believe would never end.

There were eight armed Blooey, he had eight legs too!

There was a cyclops, his name was Louis Fritoo

And his best friend Wimby the half-giraffe/kangaroo.

There was an invisible man who wore just a tie

And a bow tie person who was one hell of a guy!

There was a silverback penguin, two ten-eyed tigers,

And even a vampire reindeer,

But they were all full of love, there was no need to fear.

We were all playing and laughing until we heard a knock on the door,

And in stepped a character, we had never seen before.

He had three eyes and two tails, four noses and five wings,

And every word this character spoke he felt he had to sing.

We all asked "Who are you?" And he opened up wide

And sang it aloud, "My name is Frostyfus Clyde."

We all said, "Hi Frostyfus, how's everything? What's new?"

He again sang aloud, "I've got a card game to show you."

He said we'd need money for this one, we were unsure why

And he said he had a magical powder that would make us feel high.

We asked "Higher than churches and buildings and planes?"

He said, "Higher than Skyscrapers and cranes it's insane!"

We all took a sniff and boy, was he right,

As we were bouncing off the walls for the rest of the night.

Frostyfus sang out in a shriek, "He-he, now get over here and play poker with me."

We sat by the table as he shuffled the pack

As the pink unicorn grew addicted to crack.

He passed round the cards, and we put in our money; it was a strange sight to see a coke-head twelve-foot bunny.

I put on my poker face, and I put on my shades. I smiled on the inside as I had a full house of spades.

We played it for hours hand after hand,

As I just kept on winning grand after grand.

Frostyfus looked worried so he sang out, "He's cheating!"

The once friendly, fun monsters then gave me a beating.

I shouted, "I wouldn't cheat, guys, you know I'm no disgrace!"

Blooey did not believe me and sliced open my face.

I was in a state of terror, I did not know what to do,

I then got waterboarded by Louis Fritoo.

I could feel myself drowning while coughing up water,

They all said, "Leave him to die," like a lamb to the slaughter.

Frostyfus said, "Great, then you can all give me my money."

"You looking to die?" said the coke-head twelve-foot bunny.

The pink unicorn said, "Yeah, that money's all mine,"

He received a fierce beating from the invisible man with the tie.

The Bow-tie person put a gun to Frostyfus' head

As he warned the whole room, "Touch my money and you're dead."

A ten-eyed tiger came in and snuck up behind him,

And swabbed at his eyes in an attempt to blind him.

The silverback penguin kept running around,

The cocaine drove him crazy, he snorted more than a pound.

They all began to battle in a money-fueled war,

With cocaine up their noses and so much blood and gore.

Wimby bounced in, remember the half-giraffe/kangaroo?

Well, he set fire to his best friend, Louis Fritoo.

"Mmm, smells good," said the bow-tie guy about poor burning Louis.

He began to eat him and said, "He tastes good like chicken but a little more chewie."

Blooey ran over, he wanted to try,

He said, "Mmm, that's delightful," while chewing Louis' eye.

Someone else ate his arms and someone else ate his heart,

They then gathered his leftovers and made Louis Fritoo tart.

The now evil monsters who were once oh so sweet,

Now had a craving for monster flesh, blood, and meat.

They cooked one another, they made curry from their legs and thighs,

And made chocolate brownies out of the vampire reindeer's eyes.

They made an invisible cake out of the invisible man and ate it,

And turned the bow tie person into cheese I felt sick as I watched them grate it.

So many dishes, some hot and some cold,

Some served on plates and some served in bowls,

Ten-eyed tiger toast and ten-eyed tiger pies,

And the pink unicorn into burgers and fries.

Blooey was squashed up and turned into jam,

And they slow cooked the twelve-foot bunny, now a honey-glazed ham.

The silverback penguin went crazy, he was going insane,

So they boiled him with noodles like chicken chow-mein.

Frostyfus then opened wide

And said, "We're the only ones left, you've got nowhere to hide."

I was all out of energy, I had lost so much blood,

I believed I would die, I really did think I would.

But wait! I just noticed excess cocaine on my clothes,

I needed the energy it went straight up my nose.

We broke into battle, I was back from the dead,

As I pulled out his teeth and drop-kicked his head.

He jumped straight up from his back and hit me a good ol' one two

Caught me with a spinning heel kick, this guy was skilled at Kung Fu.

This fight was a bloodbath, there was blood everywhere,

As it ran down his face and trickled down my hair.

Cartwheels and frontflips, spinning elbows and backflip kicks,

I hate to admit but he had some great tricks.

He got me in a headlock. I felt I was out,

But I mustered up strength, and I let out a shout.

I bit off his arm, I had bitten right through it;

I then noticed how good it tasted as I began to chew it.

I pulled out his kidneys and cut out his lungs,

I opened his mouth and chopped out his tongue.

I put his two legs in the oven to bake,

And cooked up his four noses like some fine fillet steak.

His five wings flavored and turned into jelly,

And his eyeballs I flattened into pancakes, they went straight in my belly.

His toenails now popcorn, and his fingers now toffee,

I mixed his blood with Arabica beans and made a nice brew of coffee.

I enjoyed it so much, I was in love with the taste, I inhaled every inch, not one bit went to waste.

I had a craving for his blood, and I didn't know why,

And I felt no empathy eating up the poor guy.

Then I figured out, the cocaine screwed my mind,

And all this lust for money made everyone blind.

Don't fight over money, and do not take drugs,

Life's never good if you're dealing with thugs.

These drugs do no good; you'll OD or end up with a bullet in the head,

Why not do something more positive instead?

And don't mess with money,

Screw over the wrong guy, and the results won't be funny.

What good is it to have all this money to spend,

If your life is forced to a premature end?

All these things will toy with your brain,

You won't be yourself, you might go insane.

You might screw up big-time, you might go to jail,

You could end up with life and be denied any bail.

Is it worth it pumping money up your nose or into your arm?

Is it worth all the hassle? Is it worth all the harm?

The same goes for all drugs, meth, heroin, crack,

Make one bad decision there may be no turning back.

As I stood there shivering while drenched in blood,

I wished I could go back and God knows I would.

But it was now morning and the mansion changed back to a house,

But because of my actions I still felt as small as a mouse.

I walked back through the invisible door,

Where my monster friends and I had lived once before.

Now my friends were all dead. They were chopped up and beaten,

Chewed up and baked, and all of them were eaten.

This time, I go alone, and it'll never be the same,

Why the hell didn't we just play a different card game?

THIRTEEN
THE GRAVEDIGGERS

Max and Dax were twin orphans and the year was 1863,

Their whole lives were spent in an orphanage, never knowing their family.

They were told their mother died in childbirth, and their father they did not know,

They had no way of finding him, that's how things were so long ago.

Max and Dax were gravediggers and they were in the graveyard one spooky night,

And out came the long long man and gave them both a fright,

He was 8 feet tall and had a top hat on his head,

His skin was pale and sickly with green moles like moldy bread.

His back was curved with a grey tattered beard on his face,

With a long back trench coat that was tied by the waist,

His body had no meat, he was all skin and bone,

And this tall daunting looking figure came to the graveyard all on his own.

He said, "My name's Mr. Skinny boys, and I have a job for thee,

How about I pay you both 300 pounds, and you dig up a grave for me?"

And what you must remember is that 300 pounds was a lot of money back in that time,

But graverobbing is, and always was, a truly terrible terrible crime.

They both said, "But why? That's such a strange thing to do?"

Mr. Skinny said, "Fine if you don't want to help, I'll just ask somebody else to."

The two brothers paused and discussed for a while,

Then they thought how that money could help, and they answered Mr. Skinny with a smile,

"Okay, Mr. Skinny we'll do as you ask,

Which grave shall we dig to complete your task?"

Mr. Skinny said, "Fabulous boys, I'm glad to have you on board,

In that unmarked grave over there, is the woman I loved and adored"

He pointed his long finger to a grave up ahead,

He said, "She was the love of my life and I cannot cope since she's been dead"

Max and Dax said, "We're sorry but what will digging her up do?"

Mr Skinny grinned. "Well, let's just say I've figured something out, but you wouldn't believe me if I told you"

"Figured something out?" the two boys thought in their head,

"What the hell could he mean? The woman is dead!!"

The boys questioned him on it and to their surprise,

Mr. Skinny said, "I can bring people back from their demise"

The two boys did not believe him, they both thought "what the hell?"

But when it came to digging up the grave they believed they may as well.

So they picked up their shovels and walked over to the unmarked grave,

Mr. Skinny said, "I would've dug it myself, but my back is too bad these days".

His voice was posh and he was very well-spoken,

And he claimed, "Love is a spell that can never be broken."

Max shoveled left and Dax shoveled right,

And they finally reached the coffin before the end of the night.

They hoisted it up and opened it wide,

The two brothers got sick over the stench from inside.

Inside was a skeleton without its flesh and meat,

And when Mr. Skinny laid his eyes on his love, you could hear the old man weep.

He picked her up and cradled her as his eyes filled up with tears,

"My darling, we're finally reunited, it's been the most dreadful 20 years."

Max and Dax both said, "Mr. Skinny may we now have our 300-pound sir?"

"Of course my boys," said Mr. Skinny, "But could you carry her to my home first?"

Max and Dax both shrugged and said, "No problem, is your house far?"

It was a 2-mile journey, but you must remember back then there was no such thing as a car.

The two brothers weren't too happy but for 300 pounds they said "Fine okay."

They both grabbed an end of the coffin and they carried her all the way.

The house was out the countryside, so they avoided going near the town,

They would've been jailed if they were seen carrying the coffin around.

When they arrived at the house they asked, "Can we now have our 300 pound?"

Mr. Skinny said, "Of course my boys, but can you first carry her in and place her down safe and sound?"

The house was gigantic so they knew this guy must be very wealthy,

But by his sickly-looking skin, they presumed the old man wasn't healthy.

They both just said, "Fine" and Mr. Skinny swung open the door,

They asked "Where will we put her? Will we just place the coffin on the floor?"

Mr. Skinny said, "No not there boys, right down the hall, just go straight through,

and before I pay you both your money there's something I must tell you too."

They followed down the hall and they came to a dark creepy laboratory,

There were dissected bodies all on the floor, Mr. Skinny said, "Now let me tell you a story."

Max and Dax were creeped the hell out,

They let out a cry and they let out a shout.

Mr. Skinny said, "Please boys don't be afraid,

Once I tell you the story then you will both be paid."

The two boys in shock they just froze and said, "Okay.

Mr. Skinny said "Great I'll start my story right away."

"20 years ago I lost the love of my life,

Stacy fell pregnant before I could make her my wife,

I was just a poor young man, and she came from a home of wealth,

and when her father learned of our courtship, he beat her with a belt,

he said if she ever saw me again, he'd put a bullet in her head,

I decided to stay away to keep her safe, I did not want her dead.

Soon after giving birth, she gave our two children away,

I remember her coming to me, crying her eyes out that day,

And as she wept upon my shoulder,

Her father came behind and shot her like he told her,

My blood began to flow so much colder,

And I tackled him and smacked his head right off a boulder.

I killed him in cold blood, and my darling was dead too,

So I ran away in hope to create a life that was new,

But I figured out an antidote to bring her back to life,

Oh and there's one more thing I need to say about myself and my future wife,

You see, I am your father, and she is your mother,

And you are our children, the little twin brothers.

Max began to scream, and Dax began to shout,

Mr. Skinny pleaded with them "please boys, hear me out!

I'm sure once I bring your mother back, you will no longer feel doubt,

And finally, after all these years, we can show you what family is all about.

Losing the three of you made me fall apart,

But with you boys and your mother back, I can reconnect the pieces of my heart.

I know this all must be a lot for you to hear,

But please try to understand, and try not to fear,

Just give me a chance, and let me bring your mother back,

And we can all begin to get our lives on track."

As scared as Max and Dax were, they wanted a family,

They always longed for their parents and wanted to live happily.

Max said, "Father, please bring our mother back,

And Dax said, "Yes, please do father, we can be our own little pack,

And although so many years have passed,

We can't wait to have a complete family at last."

Mr. Skinny teared up, as did the boys,

And he called Max and Dax his "little bundles of joys."

He gave them a hug, and they hugged him back too,

And they were all ready to start a life that was new.

Mr. Skinny gave her the antidote, and my God it was crazy,

As a ray of light ran through the body of Stacy,

And tears of joy ran down their cheeks, as Stacy was now back to life,

Max and Dax now had their mother, and Mr. Skinny had his future wife.

Stacy was crying too, and she gave Mr. Skinny a kiss,

And he told her how much he loves her, and how much she's been missed.

Stacy somehow knew exactly who Max and Dax were,

And she was exclaiming how much her two sons mean to her.

It was a beautiful moment, a family together as one,

They played games and told stories, and they all had some fun.

Max and Dax moved in with their parents that night,

And you'd struggle to find a family as loving and tight.

Their lives now filled with happiness, warmth, and laughter,

And it's safe to say that they all lived happily ever after.

ABOUT THE AUTHOR

Glen Brady-Power is an Irish author. He holds a Level 8 Degree in Writing and Literature, which he obtained from the Atlantic Technological University. Glen is a short story competition winner, has had a play produced, and has a short story published. Glen wrote this collection of rhyming short stories over several years.

Milton Keynes UK
Ingram Content Group UK Ltd.
UKHW021543160924
1673UKWH00056B/280